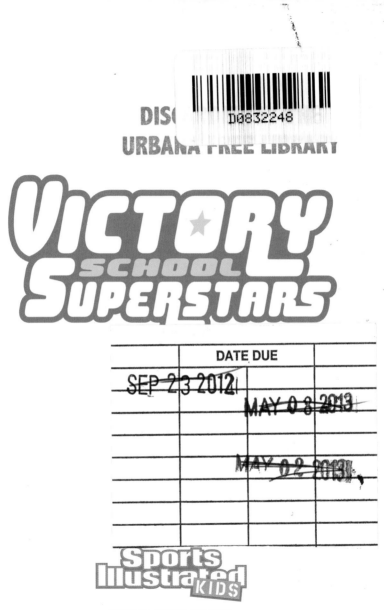

D0832248

VICTORY ★ SCHOOL SUPERSTARS

DATE DUE		
SEP 23 2012		
	MAY 0 8 2013	
	MAY 0 2 2013	

Sports Illustrated KIDS

STONE ARCH BOOKS
a capstone imprint

Sports Illustrated KIDS

I Am on Strike Against Softball

by **Julie Gassman**
illustrated by **Jorge Santillan**

STONE ARCH BOOKS
a capstone imprint

1/12
595

Sports Illustrated KIDS *I Am on Strike Against Softball*
is published by Stone Arch Books — A Capstone Imprint
1710 Roe Crest Drive
North Mankato, Minnesota 56003
www.capstonepub.com

Art Director: Bob Lentz
Graphic Designer: Hilary Wacholz
Production Specialist: Michelle Biedscheid

Timeline photo credits: Library of Congress (top left & middle
left); Shutterstock/Kellis (top right); Sports Illustrated/John
Biever (bottom), John Iacono (middle right).

Printed in the United States of America in Stevens Point,
Wisconsin.
102011
006404WZS12

Library of Congress Cataloging-in-Publication Data
Gassman, Julie.
  I am on strike against softball / by Julie Gassman; illustrated by Jorge H.
Santillan.
    p. cm. — (Sports illustrated kids. Victory School superstars)
  Summary: Alicia's super-skill is jumping and in the past she has struck out
at softball, so she is not happy about the new softball unit in gym—will she
manage to get out of hitting, or can she practice enough to get good at it?
  ISBN 978-1-4342-2247-3 (library binding)
  ISBN 978-1-4342-3870-2 (pbk.)
  1. Softball—Juvenile fiction. 2. Self-confidence—Juvenile fiction.
3. Teamwork (Sports)—Juvenile fiction. [1. Softball—Fiction. 2. Self-
confidence—Juvenile fiction. 3. Perseverance (Ethics)—Fiction.] I. Santillan,
Jorge, ill. II. Title. III. Series: Sports Illustrated kids. Victory School superstars.

PZ7.G21471ao 2012
813.6—dc23   2011033739

TABLE of CONTENTS

Alicia Gohl

Softball

AGE: 10
GRADE: 4
SUPER SPORTS ABILITY: Super jumping

CARMEN

DANNY

KENZIE

TYLER

JOSH

VICTORY SCHOOL MAP

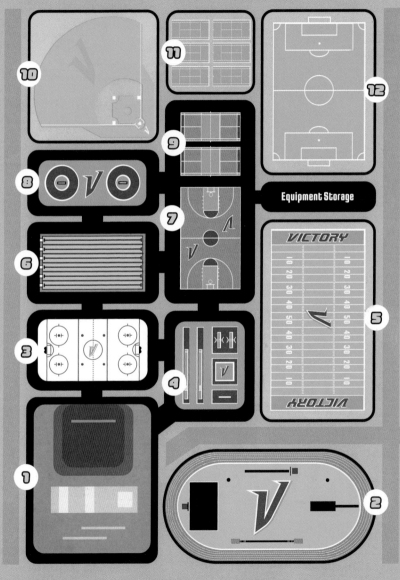

1. BMX/Skateboarding
2. Track and Field
3. Hockey/Figure Skating
4. Gymnastics
5. Football
6. Swimming
7. Basketball
8. Wrestling
9. Volleyball
10. Baseball/Softball
11. Tennis
12. Soccer

My Batting Background

Normally, if you asked me what my favorite class was, I would answer gym. I love being active and learning new sports and games. But my teacher's announcement at the end of class today has me dreading my next gym class.

"On Friday, we will start a slow-pitch softball unit," said Mrs. Maloney. "Get ready to play ball!"

A bunch of kids started cheering. They probably had super skills like super speed, so they could get to the base in the blink of an eye. We all had a super skill at Victory School. But ones like mine, super jumping, didn't necessarily help any when it came to softball.

That's why instead of cheering, I just stood there, counting the hours until I will once again embarrass myself in softball.

It has been almost a year since I have faced the batter's box. But when I think about it, I feel just as upset as I did the day it happened.

I had never played softball before. For lots of kids, the game was old news. They had been playing it for years after school. Some of them even played softball or baseball in summer leagues.

But I usually spend my free time dancing or making up cheers. Or just jumping to see how high I can get. Playing softball in gym had sounded fun though!

All the Superstars seem to be pretty good at all sports. So it was no surprise when the game took off with a bang. There were great hits, amazing catches, and everyone was having fun.

When I was playing in the outfield, my friend Kenzie used her super strength to hit one out by the fence. I leaped across the field. Then I jumped so that the ball was coming straight at me.

It should have been an easy catch, but the ball went right past my glove. Kenzie got a triple and drove in two runs for the her team.

Most players wouldn't have even made it over there, so it wasn't a big deal that I missed the catch. *I'll prove myself when I bat,* I thought.

Finally my chance to hit my own home run came. My team was down by one. Runners stood on second and third base.

As I stepped up to the plate, Mrs. Maloney shouted, "We only have a few minutes left. Alicia will be the last batter. Ready, Alicia?"

"Yes, ma'am!" I shouted back. I stood
the way Mrs. Maloney had shown us. My
knees were slightly bent, and I was tilted
forward a little at the waist. I held the bat
over my left shoulder, ready to swing.

You can do this, I told myself. *And when
you do, you'll win the game!*

The first pitch came my way. "Strike one!" Mrs. Maloney yelled. She was the umpire behind the plate.

One strike doesn't mean anything, I thought.

The next pitch came toward me. I swung. And I missed.

"Hey, Alicia, you're supposed to HIT the ball," teased my twin Danny.

"No heckling out of you, Mr. Gohl," said Mrs. Maloney. "Don't pay any attention, Alicia. You can do this."

The last pitch came my way. I swung hard, but the bat cut under the ball.

I couldn't believe it. I struck out. I heard my teammates groaning and complaining. I was the only one to strike out the whole game.

I decided right then and there that I would go on strike against softball.

Making a Plan

Heading back to my locker after gym, my friend Tyler ends up walking by me.

"I'm pumped about softball," he says. "I have been itching to play a game of ball ever since I had to miss the Spirit Week baseball game because of my sprained ankle."

"Uh-huh," I say quietly. The last thing I want to talk about is softball.

"What's wrong? Aren't you excited? Last year was so fun!" he says.

"It wasn't fun for me! I made a fool of myself," I say. "I am on strike against softball!"

"What are you talking about?" Tyler asks. He looks at me like I'm crazy.

"Don't you remember? My team was down by one, and I was up to bat. And I struck out! I totally struck out," I say.

"Oh, yeah! I remember. I was on the other team . . . so thanks!" he says, grinning.

"Ha, ha. Anyway, I am just going to have to figure out a way to get out of batting," I say.

I start making a plan. "Maybe I will just keep moving to the end of the line. Mrs. Maloney won't even notice."

Tyler gives me a doubtful look. "Don't you think you should spend your time practicing instead of making up plans that will never work? If you worked at it, you could probably learn to hit before the end of the week."

He has a point. It is a good idea if I actually thought I could learn to hit. But I don't.

Try the Tee

The more I think about it, the more I think Tyler is probably right. Mrs. Maloney will never let me get away with skipping my turn at bat. She ALWAYS knows EVERYTHING that is happening during class. I think she has eyes in the back of her head.

So I need a new plan. Once again, Tyler is right. I need to practice.

After dinner, I ask my mom if I can use the computer. I do a search for "how to practice batting by myself."

I read, "Use a tee. Move the tee around to higher, then lower levels. This will let you practice hitting pitches of different heights." Hopefully, we still have Danny's old tee that he got on our fourth birthday!

After digging around in the shed for a
while, I pull out the old tee. It is in rough
shape, but it will do. I set it up at the edge
of the yard and start taking swings. Even
with the tee, I don't hit the ball every time.
That is how bad I am.

After a while though, I start to feel a rhythm. Maybe I can do this after all. Then I hear Danny's laugh, and I know right away that he is laughing at me.

"What are you doing? Since when are you a preschooler, playing T-ball?" Danny teases.

"Don't worry about it," I say, turning away from him.

"Seriously, what are you doing?" he asks. With his super speed, he zips around and faces me again. He looks at me like I have two heads or three eyeballs.

"If you must know, I am working on my batting. I don't want to make a fool of myself in softball again," I explain.

"Girls are so weird," says Danny, shaking his head. "Sorry to tell you, but being a pro T-ball batter doesn't mean you will be able to hit a pitch. Or are you going to bring your tee to gym?"

Danny's really laughing at me now. "Ugh! Leave me alone!" I yell.

"Don't worry. I'm out of here," says Danny, as he zooms through the yard to the back door of the house.

"Don't worry," I repeat to myself. If only I could follow that advice.

To the Rescue

After a few more hits, I give up. What's the use? Danny is right. Becoming an expert batter off a tee won't make any difference.

I put the tee, ball, and bat away, but as I come out of the shed, Danny appears with Mom and Dad following behind him. My parents are dressed like they are ready for a workout.

"What's up? Are we going on a bike ride?" I ask.

"Nope," says Danny. "We are going to play softball! Well, we're going to help you bat anyway."

"Danny says you could use some help," Mom says. "You should have asked me! I used to be pretty good at softball when I was a kid."

"You were? Are you sure I'm your daughter?" I ask. "I hate softball!"

"You hate it? Come on! It isn't that bad," she says, grinning. "I'll pitch to you. Danny can catch, and Dad can give you pointers."

Everyone moves into position. "Let's see your stance," says Dad. I stand the way Mrs. Maloney showed us last year.

"That's pretty good," says Dad. "Now remember the first rule of batting. Keep your eye on the ball."

Mom lobs the ball toward me. I watch the ball carefully, just like Dad said. But with all my watching, my swing is late and I miss by a mile.

"I'm terrible!" I say.

"You aren't terrible," says Dad. "You just haven't figured it all out yet. The nice thing is once you hit the ball, you should have no problem getting to base. One or two leaps and you will be there."

I smile at him. "So I'm watching the ball. Now what?" I ask. If everyone is willing to help me, the least I can do is try.

"Now think about timing. You should start your swing when Mom releases the ball. Give it another try," he says.

Words run through my head. *I can do this. Watch the ball. Don't forget to swing.*

Crack! I did it! But my hit goes right to Mom. In a real game, her catch would make me out.

"Great job, Alicia!" says Danny.

"Sure, except Mom easily caught it," I say, feeling sorry for myself.

"But you hit it, Alicia," says Dad. "As you become more comfortable with hitting, you'll get better at directing your hits so they aren't so easily caught. Could you feel the difference with that hit?"

I think about it a second. "Yeah . . . I could," I finally answer. "It was like I knew when to expect the ball. Let's try again and make sure it wasn't just a fluke! And after I get this hitting thing down, I need some practice catching, too."

Everyone laughs, and then we get to work!

The Big Day

The day I was dreading is here. But the funny thing is I am actually looking forward to it now. It is my chance to make up for last year.

Instead of hiding at the end of the bench, I make sure I'm in the first part of the lineup. I'm excited for my chance at bat, but I am also a little nervous.

Hopefully, after I bat once, I will calm down a bit so I can focus on the rest of the game.

I'm the third one to bat. So far, Kenzie hit a pop up that the pitcher easily caught. Tyler followed that by a nice two-base hit.

"Are you ready?" Danny asks as I pick my bat.

"I've never been more ready," I say with a grin.

The first pitch comes right toward my hitting zone. I swing and hit the ball! It bounces toward third base.

The player there snags it, but it doesn't matter. With my jumping skills, I easily bounce to first base.

Lanie is up next, and she is actually on the school's softball team. What's her super skill? Batting!

Just like I'd hoped, Lanie hits a triple, driving Tyler and me home. I feel so proud when I hear my teammates cheer me on as I approach home base. "Way to go, Alicia!" they shout.

My team ends up winning by two, which is great. But the best thing about the day is what happens after gym. Mrs. Maloney stops me.

"Alicia, I was watching you out there. You have really improved from last year, haven't you?" she asks.

"Well, Danny and our parents have been helping me," I say.

"I know you keep plenty busy with cheerleading, but you should think about going out for softball," she says. "I've never seen anyone get on base so easily, except maybe your speedy brother."

I give her a big a smile. "Thanks, Mrs. Maloney. I'll think about it!"

And to think, I had planned to try and hide through class today. It turns out that hard work always beats hiding!

GLOSSARY

actually (AK-choo-uhl-lee)—really, or truly

announcement (uh-NOUNS-ment)—a public notice that says something important

dreading (DRED-ing)—feeling very unwilling to meet or face something

embarrass (em-BA-ruhss)—make someone feel awkward and uncomfortable

heckling (HEK-uhl-ing)—bothering an athlete or speaker by making rude comments

necessarily (NESS-uh-ser-uh-lee)—for certain or without any doubt

outfield (OUT-feeld)—the area of a softball field between the foul lines and beyond the infield

rhythm (RITH-uhm)—a regular pattern

triple (TRIP-uhl)—in softball, to get a hit that allows you to reach third base

ABOUT THE AUTHOR

JULIE GASSMAN

The youngest in a family of nine children, Julie Gassman grew up in Howard, South Dakota. She now lives in southern Minnesota with her husband and their three children. Alicia's softball story is based on Julie's own experiences in sixth-grade gym class. She can't thank her brother Bob enough for helping her practice. Julie has written three other books about Alicia, *Cheerleading Really Is a Sport, Skating Is Hard When You're Homesick,* and *You Can't Spike Your Serves.*

ABOUT THE ILLUSTRATOR

JORGE SANTILLAN

Jorge Santillan got his start illustrating in the children's sections of local newspapers. He opened his own illustration studio in 2005. His creative team specializes in books, comics, and children's magazines. Jorge lives in Mendoza, Argentina, with his wife, Bety; son, Luca; and their four dogs, Fito, Caro, Angie, and Sammy.

SOFTBALL IN HISTORY

 1887 "Indoor baseball" is invented in Chicago.

 1895 Fire department lieutenant Louis Rober of Minneapolis, Minnesota, adopts the game for his squad. It becomes known as kitten ball.

 1926 The sport gets the name we know today: softball.

 1933 Softball becomes very popular after a tournament is held at the Chicago World's Fair. More than 350,000 people watch the games during the fair.

 1951 The International Softball Federation is formed. The group governs worldwide softball competition.

 1976 The first professional softball league for women is started by pro golfer Janie Blaylock, softball star Joan Joyce, and tennis legend Billie Jean King. It lasts four seasons.

 1996 Women's softball becomes an Olympic event at the Atlanta games.

2008 The U.S. Softball team falls short of winning their fourth straight Olympic gold medal. The loss is especially disappointing because the sport will not be included in the 2012 games.

Give A Cheer for Alicia Gohl!

If you liked reading *Alicia's* softball story, check out her other sports adventures.

Cheerleading Really Is a Sport

Alicia's brother, Danny, and his friends are always putting down cheerleading. But Alicia knows that everyone on the team is a star athlete with a super skill. She just has to prove it to Danny.

Skating Is Hard When You're Homesick

Alicia is taking figure skating lessons on an overnight school trip. But she didn't count on missing her mom and dad so much. How could she know that skating is hard when you're homesick?

You Can't Spike Your Serves

Alicia is organizing a volleyball tournament to raise money for her friend's cheerleading team. She is excited to play herself, but she can't seem to get her serves right. Will Alicia remember that you can't spike your serves?

STONE ARCH BOOKS
a capstone imprint